W9-AVC-646

"For Veda Krishnan."
- LG

"To Aajji, Mrs. Indu Parulekar, for sparking the embers of creativity in me."
- PJ

The Mountains of Mumbai
© and ℗ 2019 Karadi Tales Company Pvt. Ltd.

All rights reserved. No part of this book may be reproduced in any form without the prior written permission of the publisher.

Text: **Labanya Ghosh**
Illustrations: **Pallavi Jain**

KARADI TALES COMPANY PVT. LTD.
3A Dev Regency, 11 First Main Road,
Gandhinagar, Adyar, Chennai 600020
Tel: +91-44-42054243
contact@karaditales.com
www.karaditales.com

First Print: November 2019
First US Print: November 2019
ISBN: **978-81-9365-429-3**

Cataloging - in - Publication information

Ghosh, Labanya
The Mountains of Mumbai / Labanya Ghosh; illustrated by Pallavi Jain
p.40; color illustrations.

JUV000000 JUVENILE FICTION / General
JUV074000 JUVENILE FICTION / Diversity & Multicultural
JUV051000 JUVENILE FICTION / Imagination & Play
JUV023000 JUVENILE FICTION / Lifestyles / City & Town Life
JUV030020 JUVENILE FICTION / People & Places / Asia

ISBN: **978-81-9365-429-3**

Distributed in the United States by Consortium Book Sales & Distribution
www.cbsd.com

The Mountains of Mumbai

Labanya Ghosh | Pallavi Jain

"I like Mumbai, Veda,
but I really miss the mountains
of my Ladakh," said Doma,
sighing.

"Tell me something, Doma," said Veda.
"Do the mountains have to be exactly like
the ones in Ladakh? Big, brown triangles?"

"How else does a mountain look?"
asked Doma, puzzled.

"Well," said Veda, holding Doma's hand tightly. "I think that a mountain can be of any colour - red, green, blue, white, purple, pink!

It could even have all the seven colours of the rainbow. And it could be of any shape! It doesn't have to be only a big, brown triangle."

"Really?" asked Doma.
"Have you seen mountains
like these, Veda?"

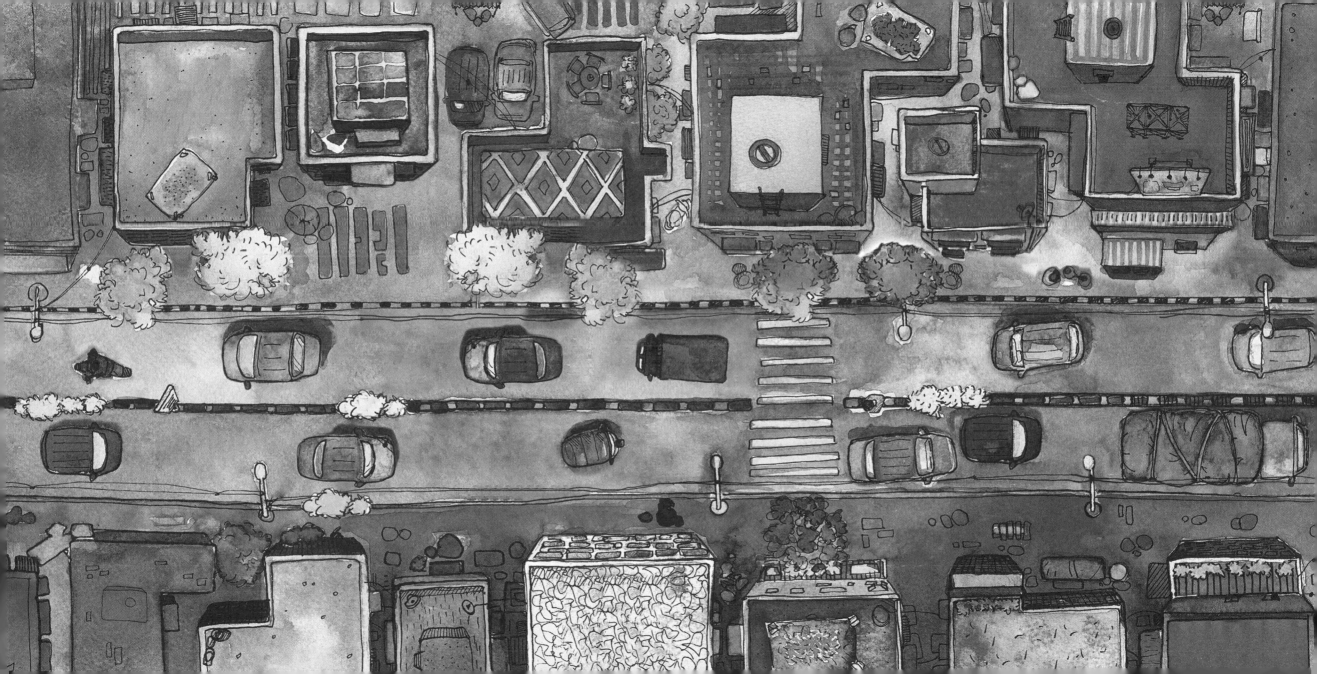

"Yes! I have," said Veda,
with a twinkle in her eye.

"But tell me this," said Doma,
not quite convinced.

"When you climb this colourful,
funny-shaped mountain, will
the breeze blow cooler?

Will your cheeks turn red? Will your heart beat as loud as the drums at the Hemis Tsechu festival?

And will you be able to see the whole world?
Because only then would it be a proper mountain, you know."

"Follow me!" said Veda.

"This way, Doma."

"Where are we going?"
asked Doma.

"You'll see, we're almost there,"
panted Veda.

"Ready?" asked Veda, trying to catch
her breath.

"Yes, but for what?" Doma asked,
a little unsure now.

"This!" shouted Veda,
and pushed open
the door.

"Doma, is the breeze blowing cooler?"
asked Veda. "Have your cheeks turned red?
Is your heart beating as loud as the drums
during the Ganpati festival? Can you see the
whole world from up here?"

"Yes! Yes! Yes! We are on top of a mountain in
Mumbai!" laughed Doma.

"Yes, a proper mountain!" beamed Veda.

"And look, a star!"

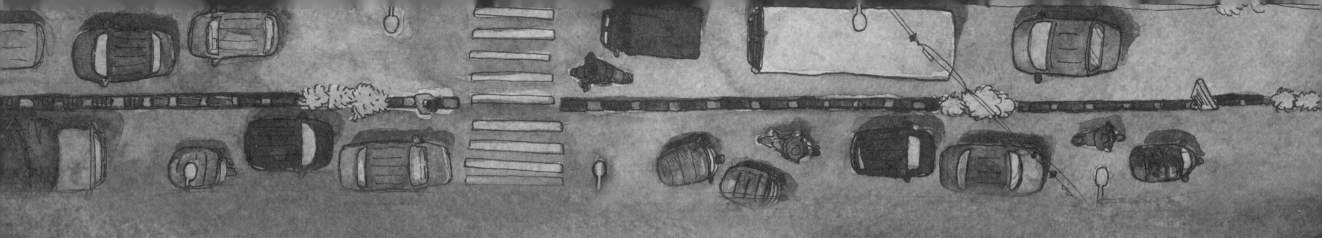

A City Without Limits

Mumbai is a city of chaos, concrete, and colour. The city will soon be home to one of the tallest skyscrapers in the world, and finding a sliver of open land can be as challenging as finding a sliver of sky. But the cosmopolitan coastal city is generous in accommodating its inhabitants, giving them the space to grow, dream, create, and ultimately, be whoever they want to be.

A city that is known for its resourcefulness, Mumbai lends meaning, beauty, and joy to its citizens. Is an empty road on a Sunday not the perfect ground for a game of cricket? Don't steep flights of stairs make for an intense workout? Does a balcony not present great potential for a herb patch with square-foot gardening? And doesn't the terrace of a building make for an open space for the community to enjoy a piece of the same sunset that it otherwise obscures? All it takes to discover the true beauty of Mumbai and its infinite wonders is a bit of imagination and a lot of heart.

Since Labanya Ghosh cannot draw so much as a line, she paints with words instead. She lives in Mumbai, the greatest city on the planet, where she writes copy for ads and teaches school children by way of work. For fun, she embroiders, reads, and hangs out with Loco, her cocker spaniel.

Pallavi Jain is a Chartered Accountant whose penchant for art, and imagination made her switch to Graphic Design. Having completed her masters from National Institute of Design, Ahmedabad, she believes children inspire change for a better tomorrow. She loves exploring and experimenting with different media to create a magical world of her own.